LOVE ON THE LOW 10

SECRET LOVE SERIES BOOK 10

MIA BLACK

CHAPTER 1

Mika

He linked his hand with mine as we both laid naked on the bed. "I want to do this again. I want to marry you without anything getting in our way. I want you to be Mrs. Harris. Will you be Mrs. Harris? We can have the wedding again. We can do it whatever way you want to do it."

I lifted myself up and kissed him on the lips. "Fuck the wedding. Fuck all of that shit, I just want you to be my husband. We can go to the fucking courthouse. I just want us to be together. Forever."

He kissed me again. "I couldn't have said it any better myself."

We laid in the bed that morning, wrapped in each others arms. I turned to look at him while he laid asleep, peacefully, on his side of the bed. The sunlight poked rays into our room through the cracks in the blinds near the window. Royce's bare chest moved up and down with each breath. His beard was perfectly maintained and it wasn't like that until yesterday when I fussed at him for having lint balls caught at the bottom of it. Beards immediately lost appeal as soon as they made you look more homeless than anything else.

I got out of the bed, glancing at the diamond wedding ring that was on top of the nightstand. I couldn't believe that we were finally married. Our lives had gone in such a spiral since the day we found our love for each other and at times, I didn't think we would make it to this point. But, true love cannot be forgotten and Royce was the perfect example of that.

I went into the kitchen and pulled a carton of eggs out of the refrigerator drawer. The marble countertops had a dull shine to them as I placed breakfast items on the surface. Just then, I heard the front door open. The outside light shone into the front room as I tied my robe around my waist and headed towards the commotion. Laughter soon followed as the door closed and when I stepped into the front room, Keith and Jessica were laughing in each other's arms.

"Will yall keep it down? Royce is still in the room sleep."

"Oh, my bad, sis," Keith said as he helped Jessica to the couch. Her stomach protruded from beneath her maternity dress as she eased onto her seat. "Jessica was out here clownin' and you know how we get."

"He is a fool, Mika. This boy out here talkin' about how he won't let our child believe in Santa Claus."

"Hell naw," Keith said as he sat down on the couch. "Look, I'm not about to let no white man come in here and take credit for my hard work. I was the one bussin' my ass to get the money to get my kid them gifts, but I'm supposed to just sit back and let some fat ass white dude take the credit for it? Nah, fuck that. Fuck all of that shit."

Jessica laughed. "See, that is what I'm talkin' about. You gotta let kids be kids, you know? Kids believe in Santa Claus, the tooth fairy, the fuckin' boogey man. Let kids be kids and have their imaginations."

He shook his head. "Nah. That nigga works one fuckin' time a year. If I worked one day a year, then I'd be homeless and Sasha, you'd be cussin' me out and callin' me a 'no good ass nigga' every fuckin' chance you got. Fuck that shit. Mika, I know you feel me, right?"

I leaned against the wall, shaking my head at how in depth that they had gone with this conversation. They were a perfect couple and even though I imagined that Sasha would end up with Keith, I could see that Sasha was the much better choice for him. "Look, I don't know, but yall need to be quiet. Royce is tired from school and trying to balance this new business."

"Man, fuck that," Keith said, "he is right behind you."

I spun around as Royce rubbed the sleep out of his eyes. "Fuck y'all out here talkin' about?"

"My nigga, tell these women that it ain't cool to lie to our children. Jessica thinks our kid is about to believe in fuckin' Santa Claus and shit. I ain't about to let it happen though. What you think? You gon' let y'all kids believe in that bullshit?"

I folded my arms over my chest and tilted my head to the side, waiting for his response. I'd always dreamed of setting out cookies and milk and then waking up in the middle of the night to eat them and leave a note behind from 'Santa.' Royce kissed me on the cheek. "Baby," he said softly, "fuck that fake ass white dude. Me and you will be mommy and daddy Claus."

The two men laughed while Jessica spoke up. "Ugh! We should've known that they were going to take sides." She rubbed her stomach. "I don't care what you say, Keith, our baby will have a good imagination and we will do our job to foster that. You make me sick!"

Keith laughed, and then wrapped his arms around her as they sat on the couch. Royce took a seat across from them and seconds later, I left them alone so I could go and finish cooking breakfast. I took out a little more food to cook since I knew that we had two more people to feed. This was the life I always wanted though. Married to the love of my life with my closest friends right beside us. Things were going good and at this time in my life, I couldn't have asked for anything better.

I woke up with tears in my eyes, realizing that everything was just a dream. The truth was that Keith was gone and he would never be seen on this side of the world again and Jessica was going to have to raise their child as a single parent. "Baby?" Royce asked, lifting his head off the pillow. "You aight?"

"Oh. Yeah, I'm fine."

One lonely tear remained caught in my eye, refusing to fall like a man hanging on to the edge of a cliff. "You look like you are about to cry. What's wrong? Keep it one-hunnid, babe. Just talk to me."

I took a deep breath as he pulled me closer to him. His touch was warm, something that I hadn't felt from him since the days before Keith was murdered. I could tell he was turning back into the man that I had fallen so deeply in love with. "I had a dream about Keith and Jessica." The tear finally fell from my eye and down the side of my face. "We were married and they had come over one morning. Keith had a key, so he just opened the door and they walked right in while I was cooking breakfast. You were upstairs asleep, but they were laughing and arguing about whether or not they were going to let their child believe in Santa Claus."

Royce burst out laughing. "Wow. That is some shit he used to get pissed about all the time. Man, I don't know why he used to let that get him so heated, but he'd be like, 'fuck that shit. Ain't no white man takin' credit for me bussin' my ass to work hard and buy gifts.' Shit, that nigga would go all the way in, too."

"Wow. Wow."

"What?"

I laughed, shaking my head. "Believe it or not, that is exactly the type of stuff he was saying in my dream. I mean, nearly word for word."

"Yeah, that was him. He was no nonsense when it came to Santa Claus." Silence blanketed the room. His deep exhales said more than he could ever speak with words.

"Did you get a chance to grieve yet?"

"Huh?"

"I mean, you know, cry. Like, I get that you are a man and you don't want to admit to something like that, but this is me. I am your woman and if you can be vulnerable with anybody, you should be able to be vulnerable with me. You were moving around a lot and I know that for the most part, you were being driven by revenge, so maybe you didn't get a chance to let that stuff go."

He sighed. "Nah, I hear you. I cried a lil' bit, but I tried not to think about it much. I was so focused on gettin' that nigga back that I didn't really have room to mourn and shit. But, it is what it is. I know the day will come eventually, but for right now, I'ma just take the days as they come and go from there."

I thought back to his proposal. We had fallen asleep shortly after we spoke about it and I was sure that is what prompted the dream. I didn't want to get married and stay in the same city. I felt like there was so much that went on here and it would be best if we just started over somewhere else. Maybe it would help us get over everything that happened and focus on the future between us.

"So, I was thinking, babe. What if we got married and then moved out of the city. Now, I know that—"

"Let's do it." I turned my head towards him

curiously. He smiled. "I know you thought I'd never say that, but I'm for real. Let's do it. We need a fresh start and I had already been thinking about it. Shit, we can even pack moms up and take her with us. Maybe go back to Detroit, you know what I'm sayin'? See what it is like up north."

"Really?"

"Dead serious, baby. I'm out this game and I know I told you that before, but I'm real about it this time. Keith is gone and there is nothing else I can do. I don't want to stay in the business like this, so I'ma tie some loose ends and after that, I'm done. For real."

"Done like, done for now?"

"Done for good." His words sounded good, but by now, I'd heard it all before so I didn't want to get my hopes up. The dream of moving out of town seemed possible, but for some reason, I thought that whatever city we would end up in could make Royce turn back to the life that he was trying to get away from. "So," he continued, "what do you think about Detroit?"

"Nah, not there. I wouldn't want to go there because it wouldn't be a fresh start for me. I want to go somewhere that I've never been. Somewhere that the both of us have never been, you know?"

"Yeah, I understand. What about New York?"

"Too cold."

"Miami?"

"Too much drama." I took my finger and danced it over the crevices of his bare chest. My finger moved in and out of the dips of his pecs and outlined the ice-tray shape of his abs. "What about North Carolina? Charlotte or something like that? I hear that black folks do good out there and I know that the teaching field is always looking for new teachers."

"Charlotte, huh? I've never been there before. That might be a good look. You think mom would go with us?"

I laughed. "I don't know. You know how she is when she gets set in her ways. Atlanta is home for her, but we'll see. It won't hurt to ask or at leats bring it up and see how quickly she shoot it down."

"Yeah, no doubt. Shit, we can go over there today if you want to. We can break the news to her that we are finally going to get married and after that, we can probably slide in the fact that she is going to move out of state with us."

"That might be the first time we hear her curse at us."

We laughed together as he wrapped his arms around me and kissed me on the neck. Royce was my ride or die nigga and no matter what happened from this day forward, I knew that shit would never change.

CHAPTER 2

Mika

Mama peered at us while we stood on the other end of the door. She lifted one eyebrow over the other as she folded her arms over her chest like a bowtie. "And what is this?" she said.

"What is what, mama?" Royce asked, curiously.

"What is this y'all got goin' on now? One second, yall are in love and the next, y'all hate each other and y'all don't want anything to do with one another. Royce is off doing his thing and Mika is introducing herself to new love interests. So, I need to know what this is."

"Um, mama? Can we at least come in first? Or are you going to shake us down while we are standing outside?"

With a crescent smile, she shook her head and walked away from the door, leaving it wide open for us to enter. The smell of burnin incense floated through the house with a smokey haze. Royce closed the door behind us as I walked towards the couch. Mama folded one leg over the other and sat down with the remote control in her hand.

Royce sat down beside me. "So um, mama," he said, "I think you know that we have worked things out by now. I mean, you should know."

"Should I? Because last time I checked, Royce, you were out in the streets doing God knows what with God knows who, putting my daughter's life in danger. And you, Mika," she turned her attention towards me, "were out there mingling with other men instead of helping Royce get through the loss of Keith. So, when you expect me to know what you mean by, 'we have worked things out,' you are sadly mistaken. Now, do one of you want to clarify that for me?"

I could tell she was tired of us going back

and forth. Hell, I was tired of it, too, but there were some things that we couldn't avoid. Those same things were what made me and Royce's relationship stronger than it was before, so I learned to appreciate them. Mama didn't see it the way I did and I couldn't blame her at all. "We are going to get married, mama," I said, breaking the silence. "We are really going to do it this time."

"Yeah, ma," Royce spoke up, "I was going through a lot when I loss Keith. Um, when we lost Keith, and it threw me off. I went back to a place that I never wanted to go and because of that, I did a lot of things that I didn't want to do. But, like I was telling Meek earlier, I'm done with that. I'm done with all of it and I am ready to start my family with her. I want to move out of Atlanta and get a fresh start in another city. We both do."

He interlocked his hand with mine as she looked on both of us. Her eyes lowered as if she was scanning our bodies for the shenanigans that we were so used to playing. Suddenly, a smile sputtered onto her face. "Well, that is good. I am happy to hear that you two are finally doing something that I've known should've happened from day one. If you two are serious about it, then you have my complete support."

"We are serious, mama," Royce said, staring right into her eyes. "We are for real about this and on top of it, we want you to move with us. We are thinking about going to Charlotte and honestly, I want you there with us. We both do."

"Charlotte?"

"Yeah. A fresh start for all of us. I think it would be great," I added, hoping to convince her. "I want my whole family there. Then, whenever we have babies, you could be right there with us to babysit or whatever else. You know you want to have another little baby around here to spoil. I think it would be a great idea!"

"Um," she flipped through the channels on the television until she got to a station that she could settle on. "I don't need a fresh start. I am good right here in Atlanta. I've been here my whole life. My home is here. My friends are here. My life is here. Now, I understand that you two are a big part of it," she peered at me, "and shame on you for trying to use my unborn grandbaby as leverege to get me to move with you all, but I am going to stay here and as long as I am here, he or she will always have a place to come and visit for the summer. But, long story short, mama is stayin' here in Atlanta."

"Come on, mama," Royce said as he stood to his feet, "you don't think it would be a good idea to come out to Charlotte? You ever been there before? I know you would fit right in. We could get a house big enough for all of us to live in again and—"

"Hold on. Why in God's name would I want to do that? I've had you two living with me for long enough and right when you all are ready to move out on your own, I'm supposed to be willing to live under the same roof with y'all all over again? Tuh. I like my solitude and I will like it even more once you marry my daughter and get her out there with you. I want to be able to walk around here naked and sing as loud as I want to. I can't do that living with you two."

"Ew, mama!" I said, wincing. "That is too much information!"

"Whatever, honey. I am just keeping it 'one-hunnid,' like y'all young folks say. I love you all to death and that will never change but baby, I need my personal space and I am not trying to lose it by livign with y'all again. You two gon' head and get married and start your family. I will be alright here in Atlanta. Charlotte is not that far away, so it won't take much to make a visit when needed. I'll be fine."

Royce sighed and shook his head. "I knew we probably wouldn't get you to budge right now."

"Nope, not even. I am that great oak tree in the forest. Nothing is getting me out of my spot. I am home and I will be here for as long as the Lord allows me."

Just then, his phone rang. He pulled it from his pocket and as soon as he glanced at the screen, he kissed me on the cheek. "Babe, I gotta make a run. I'll be back later on, aight?"

"Ok, baby."

"Bye, mama. I'm not done trying to gt you to change your mind though."

He kissed her on the cheek. "Well, you should just save your breath, baby, because mama ain't going nowhere."

She waited until he left the house until she turned the television sound down. I knew this time was coming, especially with the way she looked at me when we first showed up in front of her house. "So, talk to me, Mika. How do you feel about everything?"

I smiled. "I feel great, mama. I am finally getting married to the man I've been wanting to marry for as long as I can remember." She narrowed her eyes at me as she sat with her leg folded beneath her. She wasn't buying it and she knew me long enough to know that I was not being up front with her. My smile slowly started fading away. "I don't know, mama. I just hope that this time, he is serious about it. That's all I can say."

"I know, baby. I just saw how heartbroken you were during this last little spat between you two and I don't want to see you that way again. I felt so helpless and you are my baby. You both are my babies, but you are my blood. You came out of my womb and because of that, we have a special connection between us. I just want to make sure that you are alright."

"Yeah, I know mama and I appreicate that. But, I also know that there is no one else out there for me. Nobody. If there was, I would've found him by now. Royce has his short comings, but I also know that he has his things about himself that sets him a part form everyone else.

So, I just want to see where things are going to go."

"Ok. I completely understand because I know how love can be. I felt that at one point for your father, but as you can see, that was just for a season. I just don't want you to experience that same problem, but if you say it is real this time around, I will trust you. I will trust the both of you. Do you believe him when he says he is ready to make you his wife? Do you think he know what that entails?"

"Yes. Well, I hope so. He says that he does and he is ready to make me his first and only priority. So, I will just trust him, mama. That's all I can do. I love him and I want this to work out between us, so I will just trust him."

"Ok, baby. Mama is just making sure. I want the best for the both of you and like I said, I just don't want to see you hurt again. That is the very last thing I want to happen."

She reached over and wrapped her arms around me and then went back to watching television. It made me feel good that she was so concerned about me, but at the same time, I was worried because I knew that she had valid reasons for feeling that way. Royce had done a lot to show that he could push me out of his mind when it came down to it. I was just hoping that it wasn't going to be the same thing this time around.

Even though he told me that he was going to get out of the game, I still had concerns and I didn't want to bring it up again because I felt that we would spiral into another argument. He said he was going to get out of the game and I guess I could call it love because that was the only reason I could imagine that I would stay with him and give him another chance.

My phone rang a few minutes later, so I took the call into the other room. It was Sasha. "Hey, Mika. I was just calling to check on you. How is Royce? Is he ok?"

"Yeah, he is good. He was just with me not too long ago, but he stepped out for a minute. He um, he wants to try the whole marriage thing again. As soon as he said it, my heart jumped because that is the one thing I wanted to hear from him but while I was sitting here talking to mama, she helped me understand that I can't just take Royce by his word."

"Yeah, you can't and I hate to say it. Royce has been through a lot of shit. A lot of emotional shit and for him to say he is ready to get married makes it seem like he is still emotional. That is an emotional decision, in my opinion, but you never know. I guess time will tell."

The more I spoke with Sasha and my mother, the more I realized that things between me and Royce weren't going to be as clean cut as I expected. It didn't take long for doubt to creep into my mind our relationship. What I thought would be easy to fix seemed as if it was going to take a while before enough trust was built between us to repair the brokenness of our relationship.

CHAPTER 3

Royce

I left Mika and headed straight to the spot to meet up with the fellas. I hadn't seen them since I was released from jail because I had been with Mika the whole time. I had to figure out how to get out the game though because, unlike the last times I said it to her, I had to be real about it this time around. I didn't want to keep playing around with Mika. I knew she loved me, but I dind't know how much longer she would put up with the bullshit before she left me for real. I knew she was capable of it because she started talking to two different niggas both times we split up and I might not be so lucky to get her back if it happened again.

"Oh, shit, look who the fuck it is," one of my men said when I got out of my ride. He stood on the porch with two other guys. They stepped down the stairs when I walked on the cement path towards the front door. "Nigga was buried alive like Shyne and shit, now he back."

I shook their hands. "Hell yeah, shit. They weren't gon' keep a nigga like me down for long. I'm payin' that lawyer too much fuckin' money to get pinned on some shit like that. I'm here."

Blanco walked out of the house with a blunt hanging from his lips. He took it off and blew a cloud of smoke into the air. The wind carried it away from him in the blink of an eye. I didn't say anything to him as I walked up the steps. We shook hands and embraced for a few moments. Blanco had my back in ways that only Keith would've had it after I went to jail. He did his best to take care of Mika and make sure she had somebody watching her at every turn.

We exchanged head nods and with that, I called the men into the house. All together, it was eight of us. I left two of them outside to watch the crib so that nobody would sneak up on us. Trill's men were still out there and although it was unlikely for them to try to clap back, I had to make sure that shit was still safe on this end.

"Fellas," I said, standing in front of them. "I'm glad to be back around here with y'all. Shit was rough these past few months, esepcially when Keith," I took a deep breath because I felt the emotion rushing to my heart. I still hadn't cried much since he passed away and I knew the time was coming, but it wasn't the right moment for that. "When they popped Keith. I was on some other shit after that and I was reckless as fuck. And then Mika got mixed up into it and it made shit worse than what I imagined."

They leaned back in their chairs, wondering where I was headed with the conversation. My empire had grown by leaps and bounds since I started it years ago with Keith. We ran Atlanta and we were just beginning to expand to different states. Shit was picking up and I was completely ready to hand the shit off to Keith but after he was murdered, I didn't know what I was going to do. Now, it was clear as it had ever been for me; I needed to get out.

"So, I have to make some changes. I can't keep putting Mika in danger. She wants more from me and the only way I can give her more is if I can garauntee her safety. Y'all know this shit is my life. This is my business and I have given my blood, sweat and tears to make sure this shit was solid. Me and Keith turned this shit into something to be respected. Something to be proud of. But, even with that, every good thing has to come to an end. So, I'm stepping out of the game."

"What?" Blanco said with his top lip curled up to the corner of his mouth. "Out the game? What the fuck you mean, bruh? What you mean, 'you steppin' out the game?'"

"I mean what I said. I'm done with it. I can't keep living my life like this. I've built this shit up enough for it to stand when I'm not around. I've done my part and I've got to a point where I've ran into things…and people, more important than this. I know that y'all are still gonna be here puttin' in work. I know y'all still want to get paid and that is what I'm bankin' on to keep this shit alive. The last thing I want is for all of my work to crumble, so if anything, y'all gon' have to buss yall assess that much more when I leave. This shit is not fuckin' easy."

"Bruh. Damn. I mean like, steppin' away though?" Blanco said as the men looked on. "Like, having nothing to do with this shit again? For real?"

"Yeah. Like I said, I was reckless for these last few months and I know that is how the feds got on my ass. They know I was gettin' sloppy. I know I was, too, and when I get like that, I know it is time for me to make some changes. I need to get out before I put all this shit in jeapardy."

"Fuck. It gotta be another way, fam. It gotta be some other shit we can do to–"

"Blanco, nah bruh. I said what I meant. This is my window to get out of this shit and I'ma take it. I already came to that conclusion."

"You know they ain't gon stop comin' for you though, bruh. We don't know how far Trill's reach stretches. That nigga can have people all across this fuckin' country and you know there is a price on yo' head for the shit you did to him. You know that. They want you dead."

"Yeah."

Blanco was right. I had to figure something

else out so that I would stay off their radar, especially if I was going to get shit between me and Mika back in line. "Then, I'ma die. Them niggas want me dead, so that is what I'ma do. I'ma give them what they want."

"What?"

With a smirk, I glanced at my men as they all looked towards me with eyebrows lifted to the middle of their foreheads. If it wasn't for Keith, I wouldn't have been a tactical thinker at times. There were moments when I felt that he would slide into my thoughts and give me plans that I never would've thought of on my own. Like, even though he was gone, he was still right there, whispering plans into my ear. "I'ma give them what they want. Blanco, follow me."

I left the room and Blanco trialed behind me until we got into my office. I closed the door as he took a seat at the desk. I glanced out the window to make sure the streets were still clear. A few more of our men were still on the porch, looking out to make sure there was nothing that could sneak up on us while we were unaware. "You know that you are the second man in charge behind me."

"Yeah."

I faced him as he sat in the chair with his hands folded on the desk. "You are going to have to run this shit. I know you can do it. Yo' boy, Tre', I honestly see him as someone who can balance you out. Keith was my fuckin' balance. He was the nigga that pulled me back down to earth when I was ready to snap and kill everybody in sight. He is somebody that you need by your side right now because I am giving this shit to you."

"I figured that, fam. I mean, I can handle it. I can handle it without a doubt, but at the same time, shit ain't gon' be the same without you around here."

"I know. I built this shit. Me and Keith did, but everything has an end, fam. It is my time and I need to get out of it. But, this is where I need yall one more time. You said that I'ma have to be dead in order to really get out of this shit, so that is what I'ma do. I'ma make it look like I am dead."

"Fake your death?" I smirked, then took a seat at my desk without saying a word. "Shit. Fuckin' Tupac out this bitch, huh? No doubt. I feel you on that. How the fuck are you going to handle that shit though?"

"I'ma come up with it but for now, I just need to make sure yall lay low. After they see I am gone, then I know a lot of this shit will blow over with me and I can go on with my shit without worrying about them trying to get some fuckin' revenge on me later down the line."

"Aight. Well, shit, you just let me know what the fuck you want us to do, fam. You know we got yo' back one way or the other."

I figured that after my fake death, I would tell Blanco to go to the rest of Trill's men with a business offer. Let them know that they can link up with the rest of the organization or just get blown off the fuckin' map altogether. Extermi-nated. It was something that I would've done if I was going to stick around, but now that the shit was out of my hands, I had to give the final order.

I couldn't help but to think about Mika. She deserved this and although I knew I was walking away from something that I created, doing it for Mika was worth it. "So, where you goin' after all this shit, bruh? I mean, you are gonna be in the wind or will you still be around on some ghost-type shit?"

I took a deep breath. The thought of

checking in on the organization from time to time was alluring, but I knew what I would lead to. The moment I felt that shit wasn't going the way I wanted it to go or the way I thought it should, then I was going to jump back in and try to take the reigns. I didn't want to tempt myself with the possibility of that happening. "Nah, fam. I'ma be in the wind. When I leave, I ain't comin' back. I don't even want y'all niggas to know where I am at because I know that eventually, one of y'all would come for me and try to lure me back."

"Nah, I wouldn't let that happen, fam. I respect your decision and I know you got shit with Mika poppin' off now. I get it. You're a family dude now, or at least, you are trying to be. I just think it would be a good thing for me to know where you're at just so I can check on you, you know? In case this fake death shit doesn't go the way you want it to and they still think you are alive."

I tapped my fingers across the wood grained desk. The thumps sounded like a small marching army, headed towards the enemy. "Yeah. If I feel the need, I'll let you know. But for now, we are just going to focus on the plan. I just gotta make sure this shit is fool proof."

Blanco was right there with me, helping me iron out the perfect plan to send me out of here. The whole time, I could hear Keith's voice echoing in my mind, mapping out the perfect plan step-by-step. I knew I wasn't going to fail.

CHAPTER 4

Mika

I waited for Jessica to show up at the restaurant. I hadn't seen her much since the fallout after she realized that I was dating Trill. I couldn't blame her for being upset with me because, on the outside looking in, it did come off as some fucked up shit. The last time I saw her was at Royce's trail and even then, she didn't speak to me much. I didn't want to pressure her into meeting with me, but after I had Sasha speak to her, she finally came around and accepted my offer to take her out to eat.

I sat in the middle of the room at the table, sipping a glass of sprite and paging through a menu that I knew like the back of my hand. Shank's was a mom and pop restaurant that was about fifteen minutes away from me. Royce and I had so many memories coming here after school and sometimes, during. Occasionally, Keith and Sasha would join us and a few times, I would've been willing to bet all of my savings on the fact that the two of them would end up together. I was thrown for a loop when Keith went for Jessica instead of her.

Sasha said that she was ok with it and for the most part, it was because she saw Keith as too much of a brother. It was a hindrance for their intimacy and even though I couldn't understand her point of view, I couldn't do anything but respect it. Finally, Jessica walked through the front door. She had a cute maternity dress that fit loosely around her belly and nearly swept the ground as she walked. I smiled, got up and pulled her seat out so she could sit down comfortably.

"Hey, Mika," she said as I scooted her chair in behind her.

"Hey, boo. How are you doing?"

She took the menu and began fanning herself. "I am hot. This baby has been kicking my ass left and right, literally. Shoving his feet into my organs and shit. I can't even sleep the way I want to because of his old big head ass." She smiled, then used her other hand to rub her stomach. "But I can't wait to see him though. Little Keith Jr. I can't wait to see him."

She glanced down at her stomach and remained silent for a few moments. I could tell that she was still having a hard time dealing with Keith's death. We all were, but I knew it was a different kind of pain for Jessica. She was intimate with him and had a piece of him growing inside of her. I didn't want to interrupt, but I knew that if I didn't, we would both have waves of tears crashing down our face like runaway trains.

"Yeah, I can't either. I wonder if he will have that same hook head that Keith had."

Her eyes lifted towards me, full of despair and at the same time, bubbling with hope. Before long, a smile stretched to the corner of her mouth. "Yeah, he probably will. I know he will look just like his daddy because I've been thinking about him so much. They say that when you are really in love with the father, the baby will come out looking like them. I mean, it could be an urban myth or something, but I guess I'll find out soon."

"Yeah, I've heard my mama say the same thing about other people's children. When they look just like the father, she would be like, 'you must've loved that man to death during the pregnancy.' So, yeah, I think he will look just like his father." She moved her hand towards her eyes, wiping a tear before it had the chance to fall. "Um, I know that I've apologized before about everything, but Jessica, I really mean—"

"No," she said, interrupting me, "no. No need for that, Mika. I mean, we had our talk already and yeah, I was mad as shit about it, but I understand. If anything, I need to owe you an apology because I know you wouldn't have dated the man that killed Keith if you'd known it was him. I was just emotional and on top of that, pregnant, so it made everything worse. So, I apologize for snapping on you and making you feel like you were doing all of that shit malicioulsy because I know you loved Keith like a brother and you wouldn't have done that."

"I wouldn't have. Not even." I smiled at her and she slid her hand across the table, linking it with mine. It felt good to know that I was truly forgiven by her because that whole situation could've went south a lot quicker if she didn't. "But, I've got some news."

She picked up the menu. "Ok, spill it."

"Well. Me and Royce are finally getting married." Her eyes widened and bright smile stretched from ear-to-ear. "Yeah, I know. I mean, I was skeptical at first because of how shit went down between us just a little while ago, but I feel like since that shit with Trill is done with, he might be telling the truth. Besides that, I don't think I will be fine with anyone else anyway, so, shit. I am stuck with him, whether I like it or not."

"Nah, girl," she turned to the next page of the menu, "trust me, we were all on something else after Keith got killed. Me, Royce, even Sasha. So, I know that was the reason behind it. And then the trail and everything. Look, basically, if he brought it back up, I trust that he is serious about it this time around. Are you all going to have a wedding? Or just the courthouse?"

"No. I mean, I was fine either way, but I think we will have a small gathering. Family and friends and then after that, we are out of here."

She lowered her menu. Her eyes connected with me just over the flap. "Out of here?"

"Yeah. I think we are going to move to North Carolina so we can start fresh. You know Royce and I think that if he stays around this area, he might be tempted to climb back into that street shit. Plus, I mean, we've been through so much here and I think we both need some new scenery."

"Damn. Moving out of Atlanta, huh? Have you told Sasha?"

"Yeah, I told her. I could tell she was happy for me, but at the same time, she was sad that I was moving away."

"Shit, I know. That is like when um, when fucking Gina moved to LA and left Pam in Detroit. You know she was happy for you but at the same time, she was just like… fuck."

"I wanted her to go with me. I mean, I want all of y'all to go with me. You, her, mama. I mean, that's really it here, you know? As far as family goes. But mama already shot that shit down and Sasha is good with where she is at with her career. You know she is trying to work her way up to be the principal, so, she is planted. But," I smiled, "what about you?"

Her eyebrows furrowed together. "Me? Move to North Carolina?"

"Yeah. Think about it. I mean, I know that Royce would want to help raise little Keith and you could start over there, too. It would be cool to have you around, you know? What do you think?"

She exhaled and shook her head. "I don't know, Mika. Moving now? Away from my mom and my sister? I really don't know about that one."

"Just think about it, ok? I really want you all to come with us, but I know that won't happen, so I want to take as many of you all as I can. Maybe if you came, it would convince Sasha to pack up and come, too."

She laughed. "Oh, wait, so you're using me as bait to lure my sister?"

"What? No, no! That came out totally wrong, Jessica!"

"Calm down, I was just joking. But seriously, I have to think about it, so give me some time. When are you all talking about moving?"

"I don't know. We have to talk about that, but I'll let you know as soon as we do."

"Ok."

After we finished eating, I went back home. Mama's car wasn't parked outside, but Royce's was parked in her place. I removed the keys from the ignition, thinking about how much shit we had been through in the past few months. We had went from almost married, to broken up and right into a situation where I coud've died and Royce could've been sent to prison for the rest of his life. It was a roller coaster, but at the same time, that was exactly what our relationship had been since I could remember.

When I walked into the house, Royce sat on the couch, flipping through the television. "Hey baby," he said as he stood to his feet and met me at the front door. He wrapped his arms around me like I hadn't seen him in years.

"Hey sweetie. How long have you been here?"

"For about twenty minutes. Mama just left not too long ago." We released and he took me by the hand and led me to the couch. "Did you tell anybody else about us moving to North Carolina?"

"I told Jessica and Sasha, but that's it."

"Aight, cool. Keep it that way. I don't want too many people knowing what is about to happen. Matter of fact, it is best if nobody else knows."

My eyebrows scrunched together. "Why are you trying to be so secrative about it? You don't want any of your girlfriends to know that you are moving somewhere else with wifey?" I smiled and kissed him on the cheek.

"Nah, fuck that. I don't give a fuck about no other bitches. You are my one and only, but this is about something else." He faced me. His stern, brown eyes glared back at me with secrets that he begged to release from his soul. "That shit with Trill. I don't know how far his reach is. I don't know where his people are posted up at or what city they are in, so we have to play this safe."

My smile faded. I knew something big was coming, so I tried to brace myself as best as I could. "The only way that I can guarantee that I will be straight. That we will be straight… is if I fake my own death."

"What?"

"I have to, Mika. Look, I don't know how them niggas roll and I can't take the chance of something happening to me or you while we are trying to start our new lives together. I'm with this starting over shit. Starting over in a new city, state, wherever, I am good with it. But, you know I got baggage and the only way I can drop that shit is if I make niggas think that I am dead. That's the only way I know they won't come looking for me later down the line."

"Faking your death though, Royce? That shit is illegal."

"This ain't gon' be on that level. More like, some word of mouth shit, you know? I'm still ironing out the details, but that is the best way to go to protect us later. I'm doing this for us, Meek."

I leaned backwards on the couch. I hated the way this was going because it seemed like even though he was trying to get out of a hole, he was trying to do it by digging instead of climbing. It didn't make sense to me, but from the look in his eyes, I knew he was convinced and there was nothing I could do to change his mind. "Alright, Royce. Do what you have to do."

He pulled me closer to him. "Baby, you gotta trust me on this one, aight? If there was another way, I would take it, but this is it."

I took a deep breath as he kissed me on the

cheek and held me close. Pain bubbled in my eyes just at the thought of him dying. I knew it wasn't real, but that image was strong enough to make me misty-eyed. I just prayed that this would turn out the way he intended because if things went bad and something happened to him, I didn't know what I would do.

CHAPTER 5

Mika

"This is perfect, Sasha. It is small and it is just the way I wanted it."

We stood in the middle of the First Baptist sanctuary while one of the ministers showed me, Sasha and Jessica around the building. The church was fifteen minutes away from my mother's house. It wasn't a big congregation, but it was large enough to hold my family and friends comfortably.

The minister spoke up. "This is an excellent place for intimate weddings. We have serviced many here who had the same requirements as you. We provide accomodations as well, if you want to have the reception here in our banquet room. Now, this is a church and I know that most receptions have liquor invovled, but if you can forgo that for wine, then we can come to a mutual agreement."

"No, I think we will have the reception else-where, but thank you for the offer. We will take this place."

"Great. I will go and get the paperwork. You all sit tight."

We watched the tall, brownskinned man walk out of the sanctuary, leaving me alone with Sasha and Jessica. Jessica waddled over to one of the pews and took a seat, breathing lightly while she rubbed both hand on her stomach. "That baby looks like he is about to fall right out of you."

"Shit," her eyes popped open and she covered her mouth. "Lord, I'm sorry. I mean, 'shoot,' I hope that he will hurry up and come out then. I am about ready for all of this to be over with."

Sasha sat down next to her sister and put her arm around her shoulder. "Baby, you are the reason that I am happy that I have not gotten pregnant. Every time I look at you, I thank God for my birth control every month."

I laughed and sat next to the two of them. "Y'all are too much."

"Wait. When are you going to have a baby, Mika? I mean, seriously, you are really the one who should be pregnant right now, not Jessica. I think we all agree that Jessica caught all of us off guard with her news."

"Yeah, I caught myself off guard," she said, shaking her head. "But yeah, Mika, when are you going to spit a baby out? Little Keith is going to need a playmate because he is going to get bored hanging around us all the time."

"No, y'all are not about to peer-pressure me into having a baby. It will happen when it is supposed to, so I am not worried about it." I looked at Jessica. "But wait, what do you mean, 'hanging around us?' Does that mean you are moving out of state with me and Royce?"

A few weeks had gone by since I told Jessica about our move. I didn't bug her about an answer, especially since we didn't have a date in mind that we were going to move. "Yeah. Yeah, I am going to go."

"What?!" My voice echoed in the sanctuary. "You are coming with us?!"

"Yes. WE are coming. Me and little Keith think that we need a change. I don't want him growing up around this craziness because I know that when he gets older, people will start telling him about what his father used to do and I don't want that to influence his behavior. So, I just want to uproot and plant him somewhere else."

I wrapped my arms around her as tears fell down my cheeks. I wanted her and Sasha to come with me, but if I could only get one of them to budge, it was good enough. "So, you're just going to take my sister and my newphew away from me like that, Mika? Really?"

I looked at Sasha, her eyes narrowed in my direction. "You can come with us, Sasha. The door is always open and as a matter of fact, I think you need to come."

"Look, I already told you heffas that I cannot move right now, especially since I am trying to move up in my district. Moving is out of the question."

"Well, you can visit any time you want to,

sweetheart. North Carolina is a hop, skip and a jump away from Atlanta."

"Ya'll make me sick!"

We laughed together just as the minister came back into the room with paperwork for me to sign. Our date was set for next month. By that time, the baby would be born and we could begin working on moving out of state. I put my signature on the documents and with that, we departed from the church.

Royce

I WENT to the jewelry store that evening to find another ring for Mika. The last time I remembered seeing it, it was in the room at my condo. So much shit had happened since then that I'd lost track of it. For all I know, somebody could've came into my home and taken it because I know that I'd left the door unlocked a number of times in my rush to leave.

I was completely out of it after Keith was murdered and I knew shit woudn't go back to normal until Trill got what he deserved. I sat in the parking lot of the jewelry store, thinking about the last time I came here with Keith. He was right by my side, giving me advice on what type of ring I need to get for Mika. *Damn, Keith. This shit doesn't get any easier as the days go by.* I hoped that Jessica would decide to move out of state with us so I could do my part in lil' Keith's life. I felt like it was my responsibility to take care of him the same way Keith would have.

Finally, I pulled myself out of the car and walked into the building. One of the workers recognized me right away because of the amount I spent on Mika's ring the last time I came in. She smiled. "Hello, Mr. Harris. It is good to see you again! How can we help you today?"

"I need another ring."

"Oh? Was something wrong with the last one?"

"Nah, there was nothing wrong with it. I um, I just need to get another one. It is a long story."

"Well, I am sure that it is also none of my business, so I will just stay clear of it. Now, if I remember correctly, you chose a ring out of this case right here." She pointed with her finger.

"Are you still looking for something in the same price range, or do you want something else?"

I thought about the money I had on the side. There wasn't as much as it was a few months ago because I wasn't focused on getting work out on the streets at all. I was zeroed in on killing Trill. Nothing more and nothing less. "Let me see what else you have."

She hid the dissapointment behind her facetious, then turned to led me down the rows until we got to another case of jewelry. "So, these are our princess cut diamonds. They are perfect for engagements and." She paused. "Wait, what type of ring are you looking for this time around?"

"Engagement."

"Ok," she continued, "so, we can stay in this area. I am sure we will find something that will be delightful for you significant other."

We went through a few cases of rings until I found the one that was perfect for Mika. I already asked her to marry me again, but I didn't do it the way she deserved to hear it. I wanted things to be better than before, especially since I fucked up everything from before. After I got the ring, I called Mika.

"Hey, baby. What you doin'?"

"I just left the church and booked the venue for the wedding. I just went to First Baptist."

"The church by moms?"

"Yeah. It is perfect for us. Small, intimate and not that expensive. We are good."

"I don't want you to pick a place just because you want it to be inexpensive. I want you to have the—"

"Baby, listen. I just want to marry you, that's it. I'd do it in a little church, the courthouse, a fucking street corner. I don't care. As long as you are my husband at the end of the day, I don't care. So, I booked it. I paid the little $200 down-payment and we are set. You just need to make sure you show up."

I smiled. "Oh, you takin' shots at me now?"

"I'm just sayin'. If we don't go through with it this time, I am going to have to kill you for real. Sorry. I am just warning you upfront."

I laughed. "Aight, I appreciate the warning. But um, what are you doing later?"

"Nothing. I am headed home right now."

"Can you meet me at Murphy's park around um, around 9?"

"Tonight?"

"Yeah."

"The park? Why the hell are we doing to the park at 9 pm?"

"Babe, just come to the park at nine, aight? Can you do that for me?"

A brief flash of silence floated between us. "Aight. I'll be there."

"Thank you. I'll see you in a little bit."

After I hung up the phone, I grabbed a few things to start a fire under the sky. I wanted to do something different. Something out of the ordinary for her, and since I'd proposed at a restaurant before, I wanted to do it in another way. I set up a camp fire on a hill inside of Murphy park. It was high enough to see the downtown lights shinning bright a few miles away. The skies above were clear enough to show the stars twinkling back and forth between one another like they were having a contest to see who could outshine the other.

Crickets chirped in the distance and provided a peaceful background noise. The fire crackled and moments later, I heard a familiar voice behind me. "You know, if I wanted you dead, I could've did it right now."

"Meek, that is the second time you

mentioned killing me. I'm starting to think that you want it to happen for real."

She emerged from behind me and sat down on the blanket I had stretched across the grass. "No, of course I don't. But, I'm just saying that I could've done it." She scooted closer to me. I put my arm around her as she nestled in. "I've never been up here before. This is beautiful, Royce. I know you are not a nature person though, so why here?"

I took a deep breath. "These last few months, I've needed to just get away from everything for a little while and think. I'd come here and talk to Keith about shit. It is peaceful up here and after a while, I started realizing that I needed spots like this from time to time. A place to unwind and just take in life. So, I wanted to invite you into my space."

"Your space? Wow. I gotta admit that this is peaceful. The lights. The stars. The moon's glow. It is very relaxing, but I would be scared as shit if I was up here by myself."

"Nah, I never thought about that kind of stuff. I mean, I doubt that anybody would have wanted to cross me at those times anyway, but I can handle myself. And I can protect you." She smiled. I reached into my pocket and pulled out the ring that I bought from the store earlier that day. "And, I wanted to officially ask you to be my wife."

She quickly extended her hand, waiting for me to slide it on her finger. After a few seconds went by, she wiggled them. "Will you slide that ring on my finger, Royce? What is taking you so long?"

"You're not going to wait for me to ask?"

She laughed. "You're going to ask, I am going to say yes, so just put the ring on my finger, boy, and stop playing!"

Laughter floated around us like the smoke from the camp fire as I slide it onto her finger. The diamond sparkled beneath the moonlight and after that, I put my arms around her and held her close. This was the way things should've been from the beginning and now, it was all about catching up.

CHAPTER 6

Mika

I sat at my desk while the kids were out on recess. The end of the school year was winding down. I told Royce that I wanted to wait until the end of the year before we moved out of state. I had only been here for a year, but it was long enough to build relationships with students and other teachers within the school. The more I thought about it, I realized that it was going to be harder for me to leave than I expected.

I thought about the time that Royce and I broke up and I ended up dating Sasha's brother for a little while. The time we performed Bonnie and Clyde for the school's talent show and had everyone wanting an encore from us. I couldn't help but smile at the thought. People figured that we were a perfect match and we'd be together for a long time and that would've been correct if I wasn't so caught up with Royce. He was able to pull me back into his arms without much effort. I hated that he had me wrapped around his finger like that, but in the end, we both had each other the same way.

Just then, the alarm rang, signaling that the recess was over. Minutes later, the students flooded back into the room still sputtering with energy that they couldn't fully spend while they were outside. "Hey, cutie," one of the boys said as he walked by my desk. I smirked and rolled my eyes at him. That was another thing I was going to miss. The boys had crushes on me and the girls looked at me like I was a big sister. I could reach them in ways that their parents couldn't and for that reason alone, I loved my job. I knew I was going to make a difference in their lives and I took that part of my job seriously.

"Anthony, what did I tell you about calling me that? I am Ms. Foster."

Angela spoke up right after. "Ms. Foster, you know that boy is slow and he can't hear good. You gotta let him make it."

"Shut up, Angela!"

I laughed while the two of them went back and forth like they were known to do. "Alright, setllte down y'all. We need to get back into the lessons."

"Ms. Foster, is this really going to be your last year here?" They looked at me with sorrow filled eyes as if they weren't prepared to hear the dissapointment. Angela spoke up again, "I mean, you just got here, you know? This is your first year and you are already quitting on us? Were we that bad?"

"What? No, sweetheart, not at all. I just have to do this. I am getting married and my future husband wants to move out of town, so naturally, I have to follow him."

"Why do you have to follow him? Why can't he just get a job here?"

"Because, Angela," Anthony spoke up in a matter-of-fact tone, "the woman is supposed to follow the man. That's how it works. If he is a real man, at least, that is how it is supposed to be."

"Whatever, Anthony, this is not the old days. Women can handle themselves and if she doesn't want to move, then she shouldn't have to. I don't want her to, so she shouldn't. Do you want to leave, Ms. Foster?"

She looked at me, silently begging me to tell her no, but I couldn't. I knew that the relocation would be a good thing for both me and Royce, so no matter what, I had to leave. My time in Atlanta was up. "It's just something that I have to do, Angela. I'm sorry, sweetie. I am going to keep in touch and just because I am away doesn't mean that I don't care about you all. I care about each and every last one of you in this classroom and I want you all to succeed and do your best, no matter who your teacher is next year."

The class groaned. I hated that I had stirred such a dissapointment in their hearts, but my future was in North Carolina and I knew it. After school, I started packing up my things to take home. It was just under a week of classes left, so I figured it would be good to start clearing things out right now. I fought back tears while I loaded things into cardboard boxes on top of my desk. My door was already opened when I heard a knock. "I can't believe you are about to go," Principal Jones said as he walked into my classroom. "The children have grown quite fond of you in the short amount of time that you've been here."

I sighed. "Yeah, I know. They expressed how they felt today and it just about broke my heart in more places that I knew existed."

"Yeah." He smiled and adjusted his prescription frames. "They have a way of getting to soft spots in our hearts and in the same breath, they can send us over the edge."

I laughed. "Yeah, I know all about that."

He stepped closer to my desk. He was an older man. His goatee was peppered with gray hairs and just above his full lips, a large, flattened nose pointed downward like an arrow. "North Carolina, huh?" he asked in a soft, passive voice.

"Yeah. North Carolina. Charlotte."

He smiled. His mahogany complexion radiated beneath the classroom lights. "Listen, we will hate to see you go. You are definitely a gem, but, I do know a few people out in the Charlotte school district. One of my college friends, a fellow Alpha, is the superintendant of the school district. I am sure that they can get you into the district if you are still in the mind frame of teaching."

"Oh, yes, sir. I definitely am interested in teaching. I can't see myself doing anything else."

"Good. You have a gift and I think you need to stick with it." He smiled warmly, "so, I'll reach out to my buddy and let him know about you. I'll have more info for you before you leave out of town in a few weeks, alright? So, please contact me or stop back into my office and I'll let you know which way is up."

"Ok. Thank you, Mr. Jones. I appreciate everything you have done for me while I have been here."

"No problem, Ms. Foster. I pray that you, and you husband-to-be, enjoy the new chapter in your lives. Marriage is a beautiful struggle and I know that you will experience a healthy dose of both."

I watched him leave the room, then I finished packing up one of my boxes and carried it to the car. Royce wanted me to stop by the condo before I went home. I was a bit apprehensive about going there because I hadn't been to that place since before we broke up. I wondered what kind of memories that nostalgia would spark as soon as I walked through the doors. I knocked and waited for him to answer. The door slowly pulled open. "Hey, baby," he said, inviting me in.

I slowly walked through the opening. The furniture was gone out of the front room, leaving nothing but a large, empty space and the dining room table towards the wall of the apartment. "Where are all the things?"

He closed the door. "Well, I kind of trashed them after all that shit happened between us. It was fucked up in here for a while because I didn't clean shit. Broken glass was everywhere, the tables were flipped over. It was just a mess."

"I see. You had a lot of shit on your mind."

"Yeah." He walked into the kitchen. "But that is the past now and I'm focused on moving forward. You, me, and whoever else wants to come with us."

"Oh, that reminds me, Jessica said she wants to move, too. She said she wanted a new start and didn't want lil' Keith around here because she knew people would tell him the truth about his father when he got older. She didn't want that to influence the way he carried himself."

"Shit, I'ma tell that lil' nigga the truth. I'ma tell him that his pops was a real nigga, you know? I'ma tell him the truth, but I'ma also provide that balance for him. Let him know what is in his blood, but at the same time, redirect him down a path that Keith would've wanted him to go. I'm glad she decided to come."

"Yeah, I am, too. I just need to work on finding a spot for us to stay when we get there. I mean, we are three weeks away, so I guess I should probably get on it like yesterday."

"Shit will work out, Meek. I ain't worried about it."

He grabbed a box of chicken out of the microwave and put it on the dining room table. "Nah," I said, "let's sit on the floor like we did when we first moved in here. Remember that?"

He laughed. "Shit, yeah, I remember that. The furniture couldn't get delivered until like a week after we moved in, so we were sitting and sleepin' on the floor and shit."

"I know. At least the floor was soft."

"I knew right then that you were special because you didn't complain about that shit at all. You got them fuckin' blankets, spread them out on the floor and made it soft as fuck and then we both fell asleep like that. That shit is what makes memories and turned you into the woman that I knew, without a shadow of a doubt, that you were going to be mine."

I fought away the fact that we were already supposed to be married by now. Those thoughts still sunk my heart from time to time, but I did my best to push them away before the soured my mood. We sat on the floor with our backs against the wall, peeling chicken wings off the plate in front of us. "So um, about that thing. Faking my death. I am about to get that shit in motion."

"Damn, Royce. I mean, is that shit really necessary? I'm sure Andre's men aren't trying to fuck with you. You set his shit ablaze and cut the head off the dragon. Usually when that happens, the body dies."

"I feel you, Meek, but I can't take any chances with that shit. I'm trying to start a new life with you. Build a new life with you. If I am going to do that, then I need to make sure that there ain't no muhfuckas lurkin' around and trying to end it before it even starts. Fuck that.

If I am going to be done with it, then I need to be done with it. For real."

I hated that he was going to go through with this plan, but if it was the only thing that could guarantee our safety in the future, then there was nothing I could do about it. I just prayed that it wouldn't backfire further down the line.

CHAPTER 7

Royce

The next day, I went to the spot to link up with Blanco so we could talk about how we were going to handle my disappearance. The security guards dapped me up when I walked onto the patio. Blanco waited for me just inside the front door. "Whas good, my nigga? You still tryna get the fuck out of here, huh?"

"Hell yeah. That shit ain't changed. I'm just lookin' for the right way out."

"Shit." He picked a blunt up and lit the end of it. The smoke left the end of the cigar and floated into the air. "That faking your death shit could come back on you though, you feel me? Like, if you fake it and get the wrong people attention and you pop up later, that shit can get you in prison. So, I was thinking about another way you could handle this."

"Word?"

He inhaled the marijuana into his lungs and slowly released it from his nose, then passed the blunt to me. "Yeah. What if I set it up to look like we took this shit over and pushed you out of the city. That way, it looks like you ain't the man no more and after that, you can still come back and do some ghost-type shit or, if you serious about it, you can stay gone. If they think you don't have the juice no more, then they might be willing to just let you go. Most times, niggas don't give a fuck about shit when the leader is gone, they just want that bread. They want to keep the business going."

I leaned back on the couch. Three women emerged from the back of the house and came into the front room. They were dressed scantily and I knew what they were there for. One of them walked towards me, but I waived them off. I learned my lesson about fuckin' with bitches while I was with Mika. That was one of the things that sent us into a tailspin before we got married. "Yeah, I hear you, Blanco. That shit just might work out. How long you been thinkin' on that?"

"Shit, for the last couple of days. I mean, I didn't know how you would feel about it because of how it would make you look in these streets. Besides that, I know some of these lil' muhfuckas might try to have yo' back and start somethin' on some revenge type shit, you know? So, I was just kickin' the idea around in my head to see what it sounded like before I brought it to you."

"Yeah, I feel you." One of the women spun around and parked her ass right on his lap, grinding slowly in a circle. He took two more puffs on the blunt and then passed it to me. "But that is a good idea. I don't give a fuck about what they think about me in these streets because I won't be here and I ain't comin' back into the game. They can have that shit. We know the real, so that is all that matters. I'm down with it."

"Bet." He took the blunt from my hand. The haze slowly filled the room while we ironed out the details of what was going to happen. We figured that we would send some foot soldiers out to first broadcast the news of the takeover. From there, we knew it would rip through the streets like a forest fire and then everyone would believe what was going on. That, added to the fact that I wouldn't be around anymore, should be enough to push the agenda.

"I say we start pushing the word in a couple of weeks. I'll be gone on the third week of July, so after that, shit should be gravy."

The woman on his lap leaned forward. Her breasts hung forwards like two blood clots swaying back and forth on her chest. She slowly licked her lips, trying to entice me as the two other women stood against the wall, fondling each other while they danced to some imaginary music that floated around in their minds. I could tell they were high off some shit we had in the back. Blanco usually kept a few bitches around to entertain him and the rest of the guys while they were handling business. It was something that I was used to, especially back when Keith was around. The women's hands roamed each other's bodies as they stood against the wall.

"You sure you don't want some more of that?" Blanco asked, looking at the women while they did their best to seduce me with their movements. "They are callin' for you. They know you are leaving, fam. Let them give you something to remember them by."

I took one more inhale of his blunt, then passed it back to him. "Nah, I'm good. I got the queen b at the crib. I ain't riskin' the good shit I got at home. Not again. I learned the first fuckin' time and Meek don't play."

He laughed. "Yeah, nigga, you for real about this shit. Well," he waived to two other chicks over to him, "I'll handle all three of them myself. The more, the merrier."

"Shit, you be careful, my nigga. I'ma link up with you later."

We shook hands and with that, I left the house to start getting things ready for our departure. I had to grab the rest of the money out the stash at one of my other spots. I had about 50k in rubber bands tucked away, but that was all I had left to invest. I wanted to walk away with more, but I couldn't. My back was against the wall and I knew I needed to get the fuck out of Atlanta as soon as I could. The police were looking to put me away for a number of reasons and they were just looking for me to slip up.

That, added to the fact that Trill's men were lurking, was enough for me to know that I had to get the fuck out of this city as soon as possible.

After I grabbed the money, I went to mom's crib to check on her. I thought I would be able to convince her to go with us as the time went by, but with us being three weeks away, she was still fixed on staying. "Hey, Royce. How are you doing?"

I closed the door behind me. "I'm good, mama. I mean, I'd be doing better if you were moving with us."

She laughed. "Boy, I told you and that hard-headed girl a million times, mama ain't goin nowhere. Atlanta has been good to me and my home is here. I understand if yall need to make the move, but I am fine, so just save ya' breath."

I plopped down on the couch next to her. She would always talk about how stubborn or hard-headed we were, but both me and Mika learned that behavior from somewhere. I didn't have the balls to tell her that to her face though. "Ma, I know I have told you this before, but I just feel like I need to say it as much as I can. I appreciate everything you have done for me. I don't even want to think about where I would be if you didn't reach out and take me under your wing after my mother was murdered. Like," I took a deep breath and looked away from her. I didn't want to cry, but I could feel the tears rushing towards my eyes like flood water towards levees.

She put her hand on my thigh. "Baby, you are welcome. Now, you have given me some headaches over the years, but for the most part, you have been a joy to me and my family." She exhaled, then faced the television. "I never told you the story of how me and your mother became close friends, did I?"

"Nah. I don't think you did."

She smiled. "Yeah, we started off in the same rough spot. I was pregnant with Mika and her father was no good. I mean, as soon as he found out that I was preganant with his child, he said it wasn't his and then immediately didn't want anything to do with either of us. It was hard, but it didn't really get hard until later when I couldn't work anymore because of how far I was along in my pregnacy."

I saw a glimmer of a tear caught in her eye as she continued her story. "I was um, I was on the verge of eviction. Two months behind in my rent and the landlord had done as much as she could to keep me in the place. I was in the welfare office and that is when I met your mother. We sat in the lobby, talking, because it turned out that she was in the same position as me. So, we got to talkin' and later, we started praying with each other. Your mother was a praying woman and you know, this might sound crazy, but she was a much more spiritual person than me."

"What?"

She laughed. "Yes. Your mother introduced me to the spiritual side of things much more than I was initially. She increased my faith in the process. But, after that, things just started opening for us. I received a check each month until Mika was born. They were checks from random people. Churches. Other places that were set up to help less-fortunate or struggling mothers and I was able to keep my home. It was really a beautiful thing and it was your mother that started me down that road."

"Wow." I laughed at the idea because I never would've thought that my mother was the one that would spring her into her spiritualness.

I didn't know my mother much because I was too young to really understand what was going on, but I never went to church or at least, I didn't remember that.

"Yes, I know, it is a surprise, right? But, your mother was the catalyst behind it all. She was a good, good woman, Royce and I hate that she left too soon. I hate it, but I know that she is in a better place now and after she left, there was no doubt that you would be in my home, being raised like my own son. Not a doubt at all. I owed it to her and I owed it to you."

I sat in silence with mama, thinking about how different things would've been if my bilogical mother didn't pass away. Looking at the way things are now, I wasn't sure if much would've changed. Maybe I wouldn't have gone down the violent path that I had taken after her death, but who knew at this point. Mama put her arm around me and she kissed me on the cheek as we both sat in silence, listening to the sound of the television.

CHAPTER 8

Mika

Everything was finally happening. It was bitter-sweet though, especially since Keith was no longer with us. I thought about the night we had our rehearsal dinner and how we all left the restaurant, laughing, thinking about what we were going to be doing on our last night being single. It was supposed to be a perfect ending and I never thought that Keith would be the one that wasn't able to share it with us. In my mind, I always felt like it would be Royce who wouldn't make it to the end because out of the two of them, he was the one who was the most reckless.

As I sat at the table, Sasha broke me out of my daydream. "Are you ok?"

"Huh? Oh, yeah, I'm fine. I was just sitting here thinking about things, you know? How far we have come and where we are headed."

She pulled out a chair and sat beside me. "Girl, stop bullshitting. You, me, and everyone else here is thinking about Keith right now. It's alright if you want to cry, too. Shit, I've cried off and on all night thinking about the last time we were all together like this. It's tough, but, we will get through it. We have to."

"Yeah, that is what I keep telling myself."

I looked across the room at Royce. He laughed with one of his friends as they stood in the corner of the dining room. He was doing a good job at hiding his pain because if I was this broken up about Keith, I knew he had to be much worse on the inside. Jessica came into the room, shaking her head with her hands on her belly. "Ok, I am about ready for this boy to get out of me now. I got one more week, but I think they need to just reach in there and pull him out by his big head. I am tired."

Royce grabbed her by the arm and helped her to one of the nearest seats. "You didn't have to come out here, Jessica. You got a good reason to just sit at the crib."

"I know, but I couldn't. I know that Keith would've been here, so, I wanted to make sure lil' Keith was here to represent him."

Just then, my mother walked into the small banquet room for the rehearsal dinner. She put her arm around Royce and gave him a hug, then kissed Jessica and Sasha on their cheeks before she wrapped her arms around me. "Round two?" she asked, looking directly at me.

"Yes, ma'am. Round two. Hopefully, this is the final round because I don't know if I can do this anymore."

"Shoot, you shouldn't have to, baby." She looked directly at Royce. "Do you hear me? If there is a round three, then she will not make it to that. If I have to stand between the two of you to keep yall seperated, it will not happen. So, you better make sure that you handle your business this time around."

He laughed. "Dang, mama. You are just going to air me out like that, huh?"

"Mika doesn't have time for your games anymore, Royce. This is serious. Besides, I want you all to get married and have some children.

Lord knows I can't claim Jessica's baby as my own because her mama will be ready to fight tooth and nail for her grandmother title."

Sasha laughed out loud. "Shoot, you are right, Ms. Foster. Mama has already claimed her spot and she is not going to share with anyone. Trust me. That woman is stingy."

Soon after, the waiters began filing into the room to serve us. They had water, bottles of wine and platters of juice ready to serve to the guests. Royce grabbed my hand and walked me towards the table in the middle of the room. He sat to my left and to my right, Jessica was seated, rubbing her stomach like a magic eight ball that was ready to predict the future. Royce stood up once everyone settled down. "I want to thank everyone for coming out here tonight for the second time." He lowered his head and cleared his throat. I could tell his mind drifted into a place that he wished he could relive.

"Um," he lifted his glass into the air, "and I know that Keith," he inhaled, kept the air inside his lungs, then slowly released it, "he is looking down on me to make sure that everything is alright. Making sure that this doesn't turn into a pity party over the fact that he is gone. He is not gone, though. He is alive. He is alive in our hearts. He is alive in Jessica's stomach. He is here with us and I know that he would want us to have a good time. That is how Keith was. He didn't like when people walked around with their heads down, moping and things like that. So, I need everyone to raise their glasses up."

We all grabbed our wine glass from the table and lifted it into the air. "This one is for Keith. Our friend. Our brother. Our homie. Our back-bones. This is for him."

He nodded his head and with that, we took a sip of the wine and then the night went on. Once the waiters brought out our food, he slid my plate in front of me. Roasted garlic lasagna, which I knew would be critqued by Royce and my mother. As soon as the smell of garlic floated into my nose, I gagged and quickly grabbed a napkin to cover my mouth. Royce looked at me from the corner of his eyes. "What is wrong with you?"

"It's the garlic. It is real strong."

"You don't like the smell of garlic? That is news to me. I wouldn't have ordered it if I'd known that."

"Shoot, I didn't know I didn't like it."

Another wave of garlic floated into my nose and I pressed the napkin against my mouth harder, trying to keep myself from gagging too much, but it was no use. This time, I felt vomit making its way up my throat. I quickly got up from the table and ran out of the room. I could feel everyone glaring at me as I dashed out of the dining area and headed straight to the bathroom. I had barely gotten to the toilet before everything sprawled out of my mouth like a water hose. I coughed. My stomach muscles tightened as I kneeled over the toiled, trying to keep my hair out of the water.

Moments later, the door opened and I heard footsteps rushing towards me. "Mika? Are you alright?" It was Sasha. She bent down and grabbed a handful of my hair to pull it backwards as I continued vomiting into the toilet. It took a few minutes before I was able to calm myself down. The poignant aroma saturated the room as Sasha handed me some napkins to wipe my mouth. "I don't know what the hell that was all about," I said after I wiped my mouth. "All I remember is smelling garlic and then suddenly, I got sick to my stomach."

"Garlic? Since when did you stop liking the smell of garlic?"

"I don't know. Royce was asking me the same thing. It just happened out of nowhere."

She helped me to my feet and to the bathroom sink. The water shot out of the faucet as soon as I turned the handle. "Out of nowhere?" she asked quizzically. "That is weird. Shit, you might be pregnant."

"Pregnant? Nah, I can't be pregnant."

"Says who? You and Royce have been fucking, haven't y'all?"

"Yeah, but, not that much. I mean, we had our moments, but I don't know."

She took a napkin, dipped it under the steady stream of water, then wiped my forehead. "Shit, all it takes is a moment. A few pumps at the right time and then, pow, your fertile ass is pregnant. You're acting like it takes a massive move of God or some shit for you to get knocked up." I placed my hands on the counter and leaned forward, looking into the mirror. "When was the last time you had your period?"

My eyebrows wrinkled together. I hadn't thought about that much, especially with all that shit that had been going on between me and

Royce. My days had run together and now, I couldn't even remember the last time it happened. "Uh, shit. I don't know."

"You don't know?" She giggled. "Uh, boo, you might want to get that checked out because if you're randomly throwing up and shit because of a smell, then that could be the baby causing changes in your body."

"What? Nah. I mean… nah. People's appetite change all the time and maybe I just don't like garlic anymore."

"Yeah, or that baby doesn't like garlic."

I narrowed my eyes at her, then snatched the napkin from her hand. "Whatever. I'll get a test just to be sure and once it comes back negative, I'll be able to show you how wrong you always are."

"Yeah, ok."

She laughed and after I cleaned myself up, I walked back into the dining area. Royce's garlic lasagna was already gone from the table. "Where is your food at, bae?"

"I told them to take it back so I can order something else. I didn't know if it was the garlic or not, but I didn't want you to run to the bathroom throwing up and shit again. So, I just wanted to be safe."

I kissed him on the cheek. "Thank you, baby. So, what did you order?"

"I got the grilled honey salmon and mashed potatoes."

"Sounds good."

We sat at the table and enjoyed the rest of the meal for our rehearsal dinner. There were far less people there than we had at the last rehearsal dinner, but that was expected since the wedding was smaller altogether. After the dinner, I went back to the condo with Royce. We went into the room and the only thing that was in there was the king sized bed that we slept in when we both lived together. I laid my head on his chest. "Damn. Did you ever think that we would get back to this place?"

"Shit, I don't know, Meek. I was wildin' out a lil' while ago and I know you were ready to move the fuck on. I could tell."

"Yeah, I know. I was tired of the shit, but I understood. Well, I understood the best way that I could, but I didn't want to be around that. I couldn't."

"I feel you. That's why I didn't think we

would be here. I though yo' ass was gon' move back to Detroit and shit."

"I was. I seriously was considering it, but I couldn't. I fucking love you, Royce, and even if I moved away, I would still have feelings for you. That shit wouldn't go away just by moving to another state. It didn't go away the first time I moved, so I knew it wouldn't go anywhere now."

He pulled me closer to him and kissed me on my neck. I thought about telling him about the possibility of me being pregnant, but I didn't want to get his hopes up just to find out that I wasn't. I think we both would be excited to have a little one on the way, but I just had to make sure of the fact before I went blabbing my mouth about it. That would've been the icing on the cake for our marriage.

He pressed his lips against my neck and that was all it took. I snuggled next to him, feeling the hardness of his body pressed against mine and instantly, I longed to feel him inside of me again. It had been a little while since the last time we had sex and that, by far, was longer than I ever wanted to wait. I turned towards him and moved my hand slowly across his chest, allowing my fingers to dance over him like an elegant ballerina. I could feel that he was just as anxious as I was to pick up where we left off.

My fingers slid across the ripples of his abs, outlining every shape and curve with my fingertips as I slid down beneath his waist. He was erect as soon as I touched him and with that, I positioned myself down by it and opened my mouth slowly. My tongue went slowly up and down his shaft as his eyes rolled back into his head. He clenched on to the covers as I slid up and down his dick with my tongue. I felt like my love for him was so potent that there wasn't anything that I wouldn't do for him. The more pleasure he felt, the better I felt myself, and I sucked and licked him until he squirmed and couldn't take it anymore. After I had swirled my tongue around his tip, he reached for me and asked me to stop. "Baby," he said slowly, "I want to cum inside you."

He pulled me up towards him as I slid on top of his dick. My pussy was already soaking wet, so he slid right in as I sat on top of him, grinding, moving my hips in circles with my hands on top of his hard chest to keep my balance. I bent down to kiss him on the lips while I scooted further on top of him, pushing his dick as far inside of me as it could go. He reached up and grabbed my breasts with both hands and rubbed his fingers over my nipples. Right when I was about to cum, I stopped moving. I wanted this to last longer, so I spun around and gripped his dick with my hand and then went back down to him, placing his cock back inside my mouth. He opened my legs and stuck his tongue inside of me while I gave him head. We pleasured each other with our mouths, seemingly doing our best to outdo each other orally. I bobbed on him; he licked on me, and we both came simultaneously.

He stuck his tongue deep inside of me with no regard for his breathing. "Shit!" I yelled out as he licked me until I came again. With that, he pushed me off of him as I rolled over onto my stomach. Moments later, he was behind me, fucking me hard and slapping my ass in the process. I gripped onto the bed sheets and bit down on a pillow to muffle my screams. He pounded me into submission, pulling my hair relentlessly as if he was releasing weeks of pinned up aggression. The pain was a pleasure and the harder he shoved himself inside of me, the more I loved him. That night, the sex between us was incredible and breath-taking, and it was one of the things I missed about him the most. He could handle me better than any man I'd ever met in my life and I couldn't wait until the day that we would officially be husband and wife.

CHAPTER 9

Royce

I t was time to put the plan into action. I went to the trap house to set up the fake beef between me and Blanco so that shit would spread throughout the city like wildfire. I walked into the house. Blanco sat in my office, leaning back in the chair. He stood up as soon as I came in. "You sure you ready to do this shit? Damn, nigga. This shit is about to seem weird as fuck."

"Yeah, I know. It is the only way though. You were right about that fake death shit. I don't need to get sweated by the boys if that shit goes south, so here we are."

"Yeah." He exhaled. "You know we gotta do this shit outside so people on the block see it."

"I know. That's the only way to make the shit believable."

He shook his head and walked closer to me with his hand extended. "You know you always got a spot here, fam. Always. I mean, if you ever want to come back and make a little bread, the door is always open. You are family. It was fucked up to see Keith go and it is another gut punch to see yo' ass go right after him."

"I feel you, fam, but that's just how it gotta be. And nah, I appreciate the offer, but I ain't comin' back. Just make sure you run this shit right, you know what I mean? I didn't build this empire just for it to get fucked up after I leave. Run this shit. Treat it like its your own fucking kid, you feel me?"

"I got you, bruh. I got you."

We shook hands and came in for a one-armed embrace, then quickly released each other. "Aight, now, we gotta make this shit believable, but I swear to God, if one of yall put yall hands on me, all fuckin' bets are off."

He laughed. "Shit, they know better than to

touch you. Just yellin' and shit, you feel me? That's all."

"Aight."

After that, we walked out of the back room and made our way through the house. I shook hands with some of the men as we said our goodbyes. It was a bitter-sweet thing because I'd known all of these dudes since the day they came into the drug game. We were more than a crime organization, we were a family. Minutes later, we walked out the front door. "Bitch ass nigga, keep fuckin' walkin'. Yo' ass is the reason we almost got knocked a few weeks ago."

I spun around and glared at Blanco as he stood at the top stair with a pistol in his hand and the same glare in his eyes he had when he was riding with me to kill some of Trill's men. He could play his part to the "t." "What? Fuck you, nigga. I'm the reason we are what we are today. I started this fuckin' empire. I built this shit with my bare hands. What the fuck you think this is?"

"This is the fuckin' takeover, you bitch ass nigga." He cocked his pistol and walked down the steps. Three of our men followed right behind him with shotguns positioned right on me. "Now, you got two options. You can leave this fuckin' city on your own power, or you can get buried against your will."

I laughed. "Word, that's what you think, huh? You think you got the juice now?"

"Think, my nigga? Think? Nah, I KNOW I got this shit. Now, like I said, you can walk out or get carried out. What you got? Who is with you? Because as far as I can see, the niggas that you thought were with you are now with me. You alone, nigga. By yourself." I turned my head to the side. On-lookers gathered near the gate of the house, watching what was going on between me and Blanco. A cluster of dark clouds floated overhead and thunder rumbled in the distance. It was a dreary day and it was the perfect way to describe what was about to happen. I was leaving my baby. The business that I started with Keith and even though I was letting it go to grab onto my future, it was still hard to do.

I took a deep breath, fighting the urge to cancel this fake beef and just stay here and run this shit the way I knew it needed to run. I slowly turned my attention back towards Blanco. His top lip was curled to the corner of his mouth like a rottweiler ready to bite into its victim. The three men surrounding him looked just a fierce. If I didn't know any better, I would think he was truly ready to end my life. He lifted the pistol towards me and placed it flush against my temple. "I'ma tell you one more time, you can either walk out, or you can get buried."

A small burst of wind blew against our bodies as everyone stared at us. The steel felt cool against my flesh. I bit my bottom lip, then lifted my hand and pushed his pistol down. "Fuck you, nigga. This shit ain't over. Yo' arms are too short to box with god."

I turned around and walked out of the gated yard as a crowd of people glared at me like they were watching their champion leave in defeat. It was something that they had never seen before. They had never witnessed. A part of me felt like I was dying. The street king that they once knew me as was slowly dying right in front of them and at the same time, going through a transition into who he was to become. Their jaws hung open as I popped the locks on my truck and then peeled off the block.

I watched Blanco and the rest of the men in the rearview mirror for as long as I could see them until I drove off the block. Minutes later, I got a text from Blanco. "They believed that shit, fam. You are gold. Get the fuck out of the city and live yo' life, fam. I know you already said you weren't fuckin' with us no more, but like I said, if you ever change your mind, this shit is open for you."

"Nah, I'm done. They have seen the last of Royce."

I tossed my phone to the side and as I made my way to the condo, tears slowly fell down my cheeks while Keith sat in the passenger's seat. He smiled as he leaned back. "You finally out this shit, huh? Good move, fam, good move. You always said you wanted to get out and this was the time. Shit is sweeter on the other side, trust me, bruh. Just trust me."

After I wiped the tears out of my eyes, his image disappeared. I was alone, but for some reason, I felt like everyone I ever loved was behind me. Now, I was ready to move forward and there was no doubt about it.

Mika

I SAT IN THE BATHROOM, packing the rest of my things up for the moving truck so they could come and grab it. Royce said that he was going to come over here as soon as he finished up with his people. I hoped that he wasn't having second thoughts about leaving the drug game, especially now. I grabbed the pregnancy test and looked at it again. It was the second one I had taken today and they both had two check marks on the face, symbolizing that I was in pregnant.

I covered my mouth as tears rolled down my eyes. I wasn't crying because I was sad, but because it seemed as though everything was coming finally coming together for us. We were getting married, he was leaving the game for good and we were moving out of state to start a real life together.

I hoped that she would be a girl so that we could arrange the marriage between her and Keith Jr. I laughed at the thought, knowing that it was way too premature to be taken seriously. Still, it was wishful thinking. I heard a knock at the bathroom door and I quickly took the pregnacy tests off the counter and shoved them into my pocket. When I opened the door, mama stood on the other side.

"Well, the time is coming soon," she said as she folded her arms over her chest. I knew she was sad that I was moving away, but she was doing a good job at masking her pain. "Are you ready?"

"Yeah, mama, I am ready. And I don't know why you are acting like you don't want to move with us. I can see it in your eyes. You want to go because you will miss us."

"Well, you're not entirely wrong. I will definitely miss you guys, but I don't want to move. I am good here, but you kids need to go on and live your lives. You both owe it to yourselves and I am not going to stand in the way."

I wrapped my arms around her and held her close. "Mama, thank you for everything, hear? I mean it. I don't know where I would be if you didn't help me throughout the years. You've always been there for me and Royce, through thick and thin and there is nothing I can do to repay you for that."

She kissed me on the cheek. "Baby, just live. Live and live to your potential. That is how I want you to repay me. Help me see that all the sacrifices that I made for you and Royce won't come back void. If you do that, then I will have received my payment in full." She held me tight again and gave me another kiss. "But, you two have one more day to hang out. Tomorrow is the wedding and then after that, you all will be gone in the wind. I still can't believe you managed to wrestle Jessica away with you all. I didn't expect that."

"Yeah, her mama didn't, either. She cursed me and Royce out real good once she heard she was moving. She was like, 'y'all put her up to this, didn't y'all?! Takin' my got damned grand-baby away from me before I can spoil him good! It's alright. I'll get both of yall heathens back!' I was laughing, but at the same time, I knew she was pissed."

"Yeah, I know she was. I'm surprised that she didn't cut yall, messin' around with that crazy ol' woman. She is full of love, though. I know that for a fact."

She left me alone in the bathroom so I could finish packing up my things. I didn't want to tell her about the pregnacy yet. I wanted Royce to be the very first one I told. Thirty minutes later, he showed up. I was in my room, sitting on the bed, reminiscing about the past. "Damn, you cleaned the shit out of this room," he said as he came in, kissed me on the forehead and sat down beside me.

"Yeah. I wanted to leave it the way that I received it. That's what mama always says."

"Yeah, I know."

I laughed. "I was just sittin' here thinkin' about the first time you came over here in the middle of the night. You knocked on my window and I screamed to the top of my lungs." We both laughed together.

"Hell yeah, I remember that. Yo' mama ran into yo' room and I ducked down so she couldn't see me. I swear I was out there praying that you didn't tell her I was there. But, when she cut the lights out, I knew you didn't snitch and I lifted my head back up."

"You looked like a scared ass little puppy when I walked to the window and lifted it for you to come in. That shit was crazy, Royce. I think you were what? Like, eight years old?"

"Yeah, I was eight. I didn't even want shit, either, I just didn't want to stay home. Mama had one of her boyfriends over there. I couldn't stand that ol' fag ass nigga. So, I just came through. You tossed me a blanket and a pillow and we stayed up, talking low fuck all night. We talked about everything."

"Yeah, we did. All night."

A brief pause sat between us as he stretched his hand out to grab mine. I looked into his eyes with a smile. "That was the night that I knew I loved you. I mean, I'd know you for a little while and we hung out at school or whatever. I'd always had a little crush on you, but that night, I knew I was going to marry you. I knew you were the one for me, I just didn't know how to tell you or how we would end up being together. But, all these years later, here we are. One day away from being husband and wife."

I wrestled the pregnacy test out of my pocket. "That's not all we are going to be."

He looked down at it. "What is this?"

"That is the thing that shows that we are not only going to be husband and wife, but mother and father." His eyes burst open like bottle rockets. "Yeah, bae. I am pregnant." He dropped the test and wrapped his arms around me tight, falling backwards onto the bed. I laughed out loud. "Let me go! You are squeezing me too tight!"

"Oh, shit, I don't want to crush the baby!"

He put his hand on my stomach. "Are you aight? My bad, baby, do we need to go to the hospital?! Fuck!"

"Babe, it's alright, it's alright. The baby is not crushed. As a matter of fact, the baby is probably as big as my fingernail right now. I don't know how far along I am, so I need to go to the doctor and get that checked out."

"Yeah, yeah, we will do that." He hugged me again, but this time, it wasn't as tight. "I love you, baby. When I was leaving the fellas, it didn't seem like I was making the right choice and I almost didn't go through with it. But, coming back to you, knowing that you are pregnant with my kid and about to be my wife? I know I made the right choice. Without a shadow of a doubt."

CHAPTER 10

Mika

"Ouch, Sasha! You almost poked me in the eye with that thing!"

"Well, Mika, sit still! You are so antsy right now and you keep moving!"

I took a deep breath to steady myself, but I couldn't help it. The day was finally here and I was going to marry the love of my life with nothing in the way to stop it from happening. I looked at myself in the mirror while Sasha finished my makeup. Jessica and my mother sat in the back of the room, making sure my dress was perfect. It was the day that should've happened months ago. "How do you feel?"

Sasha asked while she applied the blush on my cheeks.

"I don't know. I feel like I am dreaming. Like something bad is going to happen before I can get to the altar, you know? I just want to hurry up and get this over with so I will know it is going to happen."

"I understand why you feel like that, girl. You have been through a lot these past few months, but trust me, it is happening today. The way Royce walked away from everything? I mean, you heard it yourself. The streets is talking and everyone is sayin' how Blanco forced him out of the game. I know the deal, but at the same time, that is just proof that he is not going back. That man has given up everything for you and we have no reason to believe that he won't go through with it. Especially now."

"I know, but I'm not talking about that. I just mean, anything. A freak accident or something that will prevent me from saying 'I do.'"

"You can't think like that." She wiped the brush across my cheeks. "You are here. He is here, waiting for you. Everything is going to be fine, alright?" I was still apprehensive. I wanted to believe her, but I had been through too much to just go along with what she was saying. I still felt like something was going to pop up and cause another delay in our wedding. She put her hands on my shoulders, "Mika, do you hear me? Everything is going to be fine."

I exhaled. "Alright, girl. I believe you."

Just then, mama walked over with my dress. "Ok, baby, you are all set. Whenever you are ready, you can put this on."

I stood up, half dressed with my under garments on. Mama smiled proudly as she handed me the dress. I felt tears starting to fall down my cheeks, but Sasha spoke up, "no, girl, you are not about to smir that makeup that I just spent three hours on. You better suck those tears back into your eyes until later!"

I laughed and punched her on her arm. "Shut up, girl! You make me sick!"

I took the dress from mama's hand and they helped me slide it on. It was low cut in the front and tightly fitted around the hips. I wondered what I would look like in a few months when I started showing my pregnacy. I hadn't told everyone yet because I wanted to wait until after I was officially Mrs. Harris. My train trailed a few feet behind me and after Sasha put my tiara on, I was ready to go out and meet my groom.

Mama wrapped her arms around me. "You look beautiful, honey," she said, wiping a tear from her eye. "You look as beautiful as I imagined you would. You are doing this for both of us, ok? This is just as much my wedding day as it is yours."

"Thank you, mama."

I heard the music start and from there, it was time to go out and meet Royce at the altar to marry the love of my life.

Royce

MY HEART THUMPED inside of my chest as I stood at the altar, alone, waiting for my bride to be. Before today, I would've fought the tears from falling down my cheeks, but I didn't this time around. I looked to my left. The spot where Keith was supposed to be standing was vacant and that was enough to push me over the edge, emotionally. I took a few deep breaths to calm myself as the music picked up. The sanctuary was scattered with people; family members and a few of Mika's friends were sprinkled throughout the pews.

"Damn, nigga, you here. You are finally about to marrry her." Keith's voice soothed my soul for the moment. "I knew y'all would get here eventually, but this is really about to happen. I am happy for you, fam. I am not here physically, but trust that I am here, aight? Enjoy your day, bruh. This will be your first, and your last wife."

As soon as the sanctuary opened, Keith's voice faded away. Mika stood in the entrance and as she started walking towards me, I smiled with tears still falling down my cheeks like confetti. She walked slowly to the beat of my heart, smiling the whole way. It wasn't until she got close that I realized her reddened eyes. She was crying just like I was.

As soon as she got close enough, I wrapped my arms around her and pulled her into me. It wasn't the way the ceremony was supposed to go, but nothing about us went the way it was supposed to go. We had ups and down throughout our whole relationship. We were an unconventional love.

The minister beckoned for our attention, but I held her close, ignoring his words. "We made it, baby. We are here and you are mine. Forever. Forever."

She cried out loud and wrapped her arms around me. People in the audience stood to their feet. Their handclaps echoed throughout the sanctuary. Most of them knew all the things we had been through and how much of an accomplishment it was that we made it.

With tears in my eyes, I kissed her on the lips, bypassing the vows. Bypassing the minister's's words that should have came before. I had my wife and our new life was just beginning. That was all that mattered to me.

To FIND out when Mia Black has new books available, follow Mia Black on Instagram: @authormiablack

ALSO BY MIA BLACK

Loved this series? Make sure you check out more of Mia Black's series listed below:

Follow Mia Black on Instagram for more updates: @authormiablack

CPSIA information can be obtained
at www.ICGtesting.com
Printed in the USA
LVHW031510300120
645336LV00015B/1098